SINNER

BEFORE RAIN

THE DEVIL'S SOCIETY
BOOK TWO

KINSLEY KINCAID

ISBN eBook: 978-1-0688482-2-3

ISBN paperback: 978-1-0688482-6-1

Editing: Lori Rivera

Proofreading: Daisie Mae - Editing & Proofreading

Cover Design: Occult Goddess

*Revised October 2024 - Location of Elijah's Hometown

 Created with Vellum

BLURB

Elijah Sinclair

Do you ever wonder what makes a man like him tick?
A true born psychopath, living in a corrupt world of
high society and darkness.
A world where a demon gives into his desires.
A life that didn't truly start until he was promised one
name.
Rain Mills.

If this reminds you of your childhood... then know you're not alone, boss.

Note from the Author

Please be aware this book contains many **dark themes** and subjects that may be uncomfortable/unsuitable for some readers. This book contains **heavy themes** throughout. Please keep this in mind when entering Sinner; The Devil's Society. Content warnings are listed on authors' social pages & website.

This book and its contents are entirely a work of fiction. Any resemblance or similarities to names, characters, organizations, places, events, incidents, or real people are entirely coincidental or used fictitiously.

If you find any genuine errors, please reach out to the author directly to correct it. Thank you.

This book is intended for 18+ only.

PLAYLIST

I'm The Sinner - Jared Benjamin
Disturbia - Rihanna
HANGMAN - Arankai
Persephone - PierceTheSkies
Look What You Made Me Do - Taylor Swift
LosT - Bring Me The Horizon
Blank Space - I Prevail
We Found Love - Rihanna

Spotify Playlist

ELIJAH

Most people would start out by saying, I wasn't always this way. Situations and circumstances molded me into the person I became.

Not me.

I was born like this.

ONE

ELIJAH - AGE FIVE

BOZEMAN, MONTANA

"What's the best way to kill someone?"

The commotion around me stops.

The table full of my father's high-society business friends goes completely silent. As I look up to see everyone has stopped talking, I notice that all eyes are on me. The five year old at the end of the table eating his lamb, asking a simple and logical question.

Shrugging my shoulders, I slide my fork into my mouth and continue eating my meal.

"Why do you ask?" My dad asks with a mixture of curiosity and concern.

"I've always wondered. If you slice an important vein, they will die quickly, but the mess might not be worth it. Which made me think..." Pausing my thoughts as I take another bite of lamb. "Is poison the way to go?"

A few of the older men chuckle, but I'm unsure why. I didn't tell a joke, did I?

I slide back on my chair, and my back arches slightly due to my wooden bat resting behind me. I never go anywhere without it. When I asked my dad to get me one last year, he did, no questions asked. Perhaps he should have asked one, *what is it for?*

Since my earliest memory, I have always recalled looking at a person and picturing beating them to death and how I would do it, should they annoy me. How with a simple stupid question or statement, bashing their heads in would bring me the greatest satisfaction. Hit after hit, blood splattering on my face, the crack of the skull and bones in their face, and seeing life leave their eyes.

Thinking of it now brings the biggest smile to my face; my breathing has gotten heavier, and my eyes are wider. What I would give to be able to do that right now, with my bat, to those who just laughed at a joke I know I did not tell.

My dad interrupts my daydream, "Elijah, what's going on?"

A piece of my black hair falls over my forehead. I use the back of my hand to wipe it away. "I was just picturing what it would be like to use my bat on someone."

Dad stands up instantly after my statement. "Alright men, if you will excuse my son and I."

Grumbles of understanding are reciprocated as my dad walks over to me. "Elijah, my office. Let's go."

"Take it easy on the kid. We can use someone like him." One of the guys says to my dad. My eyes drift towards the man. *What is he talking about?*

My dad's response is a simple nod of acknowledgment.

Confused, I place the napkin which was on my lap over my plate. I hop off the chair, which is massive for my five-year-old self, and grip my bat, taking it with me as I follow my dad out of the dining room.

Following him down the hall, my bat drags behind me on the fancy throw rugs, turning into his office. He closes the door behind us.

"Take a seat, talk to me. What's going on in that bright little head of yours?"

Jumping on his brown leather couch, he sits next to me, watching me and waiting for my response.

My bat is between my legs, which hang over the edge of the seat. Twisting it in my hands, I think, how should I answer this?

Honestly or deny any thoughts or dreams I've had about the subject.

With a heavy sigh, I begin, "Remember that nanny you hired for me when I was three? That really old lady who would shake her finger in my face while telling me what a naughty boy I was for playing in the woods after dark?"

My dad nods as I continue, "The entire time her finger was in my face, all I could think about was biting it off. And once it was bitten off, I wanted to shove it down her throat for her to choke on and die, while holding her down."

As I tell him my thoughts, I keep my focus on him. Dad's body language doesn't change, his facial expressions remain neutral.

I'm telling him my deepest, darkest thoughts, and he isn't reacting. I don't understand.

"I never want you to think that your thoughts or daydreams aren't normal. They are, for you. This may surprise you, but you are not alone. A few men at that table out there have the same thoughts as you."

His words alleviate an incredible weight off my shoulders.

My dad understands me. He gets me. He isn't going to try to change me or send me away.

I am not alone. I am normal.

My feelings are being validated instead of silenced. Something I didn't anticipate when I decided to go the honest route. I thought for sure I would get in trouble and have my bat taken away.

"It's getting harder and harder to not act on them, Dad." Looking down at my hands, I confess nervously.

My dad's hand touches my shoulder. "I am here for you. I will help you with the urges."

A strange emotion washes over me quickly and leaves me just as fast as the words leave my lips in a hoarse whisper, "Thank you."

CHAPTER
TWO
ELIJAH - SEVENTH BIRTHDAY

"Elijah, turn the handle."

My eyes concentrate on the person lying on the table, his limbs tied to each corner. His eyes water. His lips move, but no spoken words escape, *'Please help me.'*

Why does he think I would help him? Turning my head, confused, my brows furrow trying to understand.

"Elijah!"

Adam's strong, stern voice startles me as his hand grips my shoulder, "What's wrong?"

Shaking my head, "He asked me to help him. Why?"

A chuckle follows after my question, "Because he is a dumb piece of shit. He doesn't get you, don't give a fuck about him. He thinks he can pull on your heartstrings and play them like a fucking violin. This motherfucker doesn't know your frontal cortex doesn't respond to this shit. He's about to learn just who the fuck you are. Elijah Sinclair."

As Adam says my name, the man on the table's eyes widen. "No, no, no."

My hands grip the table's turn handle – each corner of the table has one – as I continue to observe the man in front of me. His facial expressions continue to change with each of my movements.

From pleading to anger.

As I turn the handle, the rope tied around his wrist goes from sitting loosely to tightened. Then, as I continue, it begins to retract.

His face was angry and now shows pain.

Interesting.

Continuing to turn, the rope pulls, causing a strain on his shoulder joint.

Now he is screaming.

My hands move faster, wanting to see what will happen next. It gets harder to turn as the tension on the rope tightens. Adam's hands grip over mine, pride wants me to shake him off, but I know if I am going to make this work, I need his strength.

One more hard turn and the sound I have been craving to hear happens, and quickly. The shoulder dislocates, popping directly out of the socket. Adam lets go as I turn the handle by myself again now that there is less tension. Then the scream of terror and extreme pain follows. Smiling, I keep going.

Loud tears can faintly be heard next. His arm muscles and ligaments are now completely detached.

Adrenaline and pride fill my chest.

Three more to go.

A couple of hours later, all limbs are completely detached. He passed out a few times, but Adam showed me that by using doses of adrenaline, which we stabbed into his chest, they wake up, forcing them to continue feeling the pain we are inflicting.

We gave this guy two doses.

He has been crying most of the time, which I have found to be the most annoying part of this. But as time continues to pass, I am able to zone out and only hear the ropes brushing on the table, the creeks of the handle as I turn it and the pops of the limbs becoming detached.

Looking over my shoulder, my wooden bat is propped against the counter. I desperately want to use it each time a cry or scream makes its way into my happy place. But the long game is what matters, so Adam says.

My dad says I have to listen to him, or else he will take Adam away from me.

So my bat remains behind me.

"Elijah. It's time. End it."

The guy lying on the table is nothing more than a torso with a head.

I never asked what he did to deserve this. I don't care, frankly.

Looking down, I see a tin bucket with a few rats inside that haven't eaten in a day or two. I reach down and grip the thin, cool handle. The rats scurry, one even goes on its hind legs in an effort to get free.

Walking up to the man's face, I take him in once more. His eyes are barely open, with dry tears on his cheeks.

Adam passes me a thick rectangle tin cover for the bucket. Placing it on top, I hold it tightly to ensure the rats stay secured as I flip the bucket over. The rats fall on the tin lid.

Quickly, I place it on the guy's face, holding the bucket with all my strength as I rapidly slid the lid out from beneath it.

Adam passes me a BBQ lighter. Flicking it on, I heat the metal bucket.

The rats become quiet.

They are trying to escape by eating through his flesh and eyes.

"You should put a glove on, or your hand will burn," Adam suggests while placing a heat-resistant glove next to me. I shake my head. I don't need it.

I do wish I could see through this bucket though, and watch the rats eat this fucker alive.

The heat is warm against my hand. Little squeaks from the rats can be heard alongside painful moans from the guy.

Minutes pass.

I am still entranced by the sight before me. Allowing my eyes to slide down the man's body, I watch his chest. His breathing had been faint after the last dose of adrenaline, so I had been monitoring it while the rats have been eating his face.

My eyes don't blink as I watch and wait.

The cries have stopped. And so has his heart.

He's gone.

Lifting the bucket up, and dropping it to my feet, the rats scurry.

Blood trickles from both eyes. Both eyelids have been chewed through, and pieces of the eyeballs are gone. The lips are also chewed to shit along with the nostrils on the nose. Deep scratches decorate each cheek. Burn marks line the perimeter of his face from the scorching heat of the bucket.

I did this.

Pride fills me.

"Now, clean up your mess."

Adam leaves.

This was my first full-cycle kill. From grabbing him, torturing him, keeping him alive, killing, and now disposing of the body.

Familiar footsteps come from behind me just as I am about to get started on dismembering.

It's my dad.

His hands rest gently on my shoulders. "Happy birthday, son. I hope you liked your gift."

THREE
ELIJAH - AGE TEN

Today, I made a decision that will change my life forever.

Not instantly.

It will take years to reveal itself.

I won't realize I have met my future until she is in front of me. Her name will send me into an absolute obsession, and her beauty will solidify my life's purpose.

Today, I have started on that trajectory. I decided to go with my mom and her new husband. I'm leaving my dad behind here in Montana. Our large home with everything I have ever needed or wanted at my disposal. The acres of land, which is home to many secrets and bodies. My dad has never limited me. My stepfather has no fucking idea what he's getting with me. My mom is a follower, mindless, and never has been able to process a thought of her own. Even cheating on my dad was probably that dumb fucks idea.

My dad wasn't perfect either. Just this year, I started watching him with the much younger females he would bring back to the estate in the late hours of the night.

The bright moon would shine into his home office through the floor-to-ceiling windows. Dad would have them bent over his desk, fucking them hard and fast from behind. Their tits would bounce as moans escaped their mouths. My body tingled as I watched. Never in all my days had I felt this sensation. Seeing these females in such a state aroused me. At first, I would squeeze my dick, begging for it to stop as I watched. Until one day, I decided to see what would happen if I acted on my body's reactions. My hand wrapped tightly around my cock, jerking it just as fast and hard as he was fucking them, chasing the release my body had been taunting me with. My cum would cover my hand and sometimes leave a stain on the carpet outside his office. I wouldn't clean it up. He never questioned it. But it would always be gone the next time I came to watch.

Even though I got off on it, rarely did I ever believe she was getting off from it, he used them for his own needs before kicking them out.

Before leaving, the girls would take their time, hoping my dad would ask them to stay– desperate, really. It was never going to happen.

He would give them an envelope of cash, thank them for their time, and have his driver ready outside to take them away. He would usually force them to sign an NDA before leaving the property.

He is where I learned sex from.

Not that I needed to be taught meaningless sex. Dad simply reinforced that how I felt about people and things was normal. To have no emotion behind something wasn't shameful.

The difference between my dad and mom is that he always stayed. Sure, he fucked around, I'm sure my pill-popping mother did the same. But he fucking stayed.

My dad will be fine. His work will keep him busy. The whores will keep him occupied.

He will miss me. Maybe I will miss him. But I doubt it. That would be widely out of character for me.

My dad, before all this shit went down, was showing me pieces of the business and how my tendencies made me an asset early on.

Perhaps you can call it a family business. It has been in our family for generations. It's our birthright to join. No questions. If you decline such responsibilities, your day will come.

You will be six feet under with the rest of the sorry bastards in these woods.

I am leaving with my mom because I know I will be back. I know my dad will be okay.

Will I miss the freedom of satisfying my urges and my needs? Yes. Fuck yes.

My dad gets me. His men get me.

But like the rest of them, I need a taste of the outside world before I am stuck here. I have ten years to experience life outside of Bozeman. As much as my mom disgusts me, this is the only opportunity I will have.

I'm standing outside in the backyard, staring at the tree line, which holds many secrets and bodies. Many of which I have put there.

"Elijah, let's go." My mom shouts from behind me.

Taking one last breath of the fresh Montana air, a chill latches onto my once warm skin. As I blow it out, a cloudy fog forms before me. Dash, the family German Shepard, steps forward and sits next to me.

Bringing my fingers to his head, I rub his soft coat for possibly the last time. He is older, I doubt he will be here when I get back.

"I'll make sure you are buried here, boy. You're family. You deserve to be kept close." I promise.

"Elijah Sinclair, get your ass moving!" Her voice is like nails against a chalkboard.

Lifting my other hand in the air, I salute her with my middle finger.

"I'll come when I am fucking ready."

Dash doesn't move, he isn't startled. He is loyal to me and my dad. Dash even got in on some of the action with us. Sinking his teeth into the human flesh of our enemy was always his favorite. As a treat, I would keep a few limbs in the freezer and gift them to Dash when he had been an extra good boy, which was weekly. He is the only thing that I have ever cared about. His loyalty towards me and my dad was always reciprocated.

"Keep helping Dad. I know you like it, and so does he."

I give Dash one last scratch before turning around in the yard and walking towards the house.

A mix of old stone and cabin logs. A giant wrap-around deck encompassing the entire second floor. But I don't look up at it. That is where I know my mother's voice is coming from.

Fuck her.

I'm not mad at her. Leaving is my choice. But it doesn't mean I like her because I am going. This is my one chance at life outside of this place before I come back.

Walking onto the stone patio, I turn around once more. Dash is unmoved. The trees are decorated in fall leaves, with the silhouettes of mountain peaks around him in the distance.

Picking up my wooden bat, which was resting against the outdoor fireplace, I rotate it in my hand a couple of times before I walk around the house to the front.

"See you later, Montana. I'll be seeing you."

FOUR

ELIJAH - AGE TEN

BLACKWOOD, NC

It didn't take me long to discover my new stepfather was a fucking cult leader. I am always observing, even when they think I'm not. Pretending to be asleep, making them feel safe to talk when it wasn't.

Information is power. You would be a fucking moron if you thought otherwise.

One month is all it took.

At first, when we moved to this hot and humid state, I wasn't used to it. I stayed inside, where the A/C blew twenty-four-seven, which got boring fast. But I was not about to go outside. The heat was hot, sticky, and uncomfortable. My body was still used to the dry climate of the mountains.

But I was getting antsy. My tendencies hadn't been utilized for thirty fucking days.

Something my body craves was being withheld. My skin itches with withdrawal symptoms. Saliva filled my mouth at the thought of ending another's life. Dismembering them. Torturing. Biting my own lip would ignite the familiar copper taste on my tongue. It satisfied the urge in the short term, but it would never be enough.

Bored in my thoughts, it is time to snoop.

Starting upstairs, I make my way through the spare rooms of this large home, nothing of interest catching my attention.

It wasn't until I made my way through my mom and her dumb fuck husband's room, that I found something of interest. Standing in the doorframe of their walk-in closet, something doesn't fit in here. Something piques my interest. Immediately they stand out, these cliche black robes with gold trim hanging in their closet with white plain face masks with gold designs tied around the same hanger.

Stepping closer, brushing my hand against the soft fabric, a smirk forms on my lips.

What do we have here?

Bringing the dark fabric to my nose, the immediate smell of smoke invades my senses.

Interesting.

"You could be a great asset to The Chapel, son."

The deep voice of a prick I have no use for fills the silence.

Letting go of the robe, I turn around. Not one guilty feeling of being caught, because why would I?

Very annoyed though, I'm not done.

Snapping back at the imbecile, "I'm not your son."

He nods his head down, chuckling, amused by my response.

Looking back up at me, he takes a step in. "I have heard of your talents."

What's his angle here?

Not responding, I let him give me information while giving him nothing in return.

"In the circles I run in, it's no secret what happens up in those Rocky Mountains."

My face remains expressionless, my arms crossed as I lean against the wardrobe. "Go on, tell me what happens then."

"Your last name means you have reach. You have access. You, along with other very wealthy families in that area, can get away with anything." He has yet to tell me what happens. I wait in silence for him to continue.

He shakes his finger at me. "Smart boy."

Yes, and I will always be smarter than you, Maxton, even at the age of ten. My eyes linger on his exposed arm. A small black tattoo, the outline of bat wings, catches my attention, as if they are coming out of his skin.

Noted.

Maxton interrupts my observations with his authoritative tone, "People go missing. People never get found. And I have heard you are very much a part of this. You may not be the one in charge of it, but you are someone who helps to ensure they are never found."

My dad saw at an early age what an asset I would be. After that dinner when I was five, he assigned me a mentor who started by teaching me how to torture, dismember, and dispose of people.

The fundamentals.

Most would think killing is the most important thing, but it's not. It's how to extract information, remind them of what naughty individuals they have been, and watch them realize they are never getting out of here. The defeat that washes over their faces each time always makes me smile.

Then, once they are dead.

If we don't want them to be found, dismemberment is key. The smaller the pieces, the quicker they decompose in the small hole we have put them in. All the tiny critters that roam the soil feast on their organs, skin, and eyes. Typically, we dispose of said people in my fucking backyard. Deep within the forest that resides on acres of my dad's property.

Once, my mentor Adam advised my dad that I was up to his high standard, which didn't take long. I fucking thrived in that environment, he built my own torture shed on the property.

The floor is white tile with a drain in the middle. The walls are lined with stainless steel cabinets and countertops, along with a sink. It has everything a boy could want.

Knee splitter, hammers, pliers, bone cutters, and a table with restraints.

My dick gets hard thinking about it now. I fucking miss it.

Next, I was shown how to kill.

If I need to end them quickly or if we need to prolong the agony.

The slow burn was becoming a favorite of mine.

It goes hand-in-hand with torture. Watching the phases of realization wash over their faces. Then the begging and pleading comes next. Which always makes me laugh. People show their true selves before they die. It's always the most pathetic version of themselves. What people would say or do to stay alive.

I had the idea just before my seventh birthday, when I added the wheel to my table which controls the restraints. With each turn, it pulls on their limbs. The pain becomes unbearable as the limbs begin to disconnect. Popping noises from it fill the space alongside the screams.

Then, I leave them like this for hours or days even depending on how annoying I find them. Only to come back later to finish the job. The limbs detach, but the body is still very much alive as they bleed out, which only results in their death.

Sometimes I play along, giving them a glimmer of hope, just to watch their faces drop once I take it away. Severing the femoral artery would cause blood to gush out rapidly. Hands and legs are restrained as they watch their own ending.

Shivers begin as they get cold from all the blood leaving them. Then the heart stops, with nothing more to pump through it.

We had just begun the hunting and kidnapping months before I left. But I was getting good at it. And I was eager to continue honing my skills. It's part of what I crave.

This is all a piece of me now.

Never did I think the withdrawal would be this intense. Thinking about it in such detail is only torturing myself.

My body language doesn't change while looking at him, unamused. Another skill I am very fucking good at. Even with all these vivid images floating through my mind.

The curious mind I have, I continue to observe him instead.

Come on old man, keep talking.

"I can give you what you need, but in return, you must help me. And The Chapel."

Here we go.

"Go on." Intrigued by his proposition.

"I am a vessel for the Devil, The Dark One, if you will. He communicates through me who is a threat and we remove them. We do not see age, race, or gender. We see good and evil. We eliminate the evil that threatens us and our work, our purpose within The Chapel. Do you understand?"

Interesting.

"The person we have now assisting in such efforts is sloppy. Because of that, curious minds have been snooping, civilians, the police. They are causing us headaches. They are becoming additional threats we do not desire. Perhaps you could work with our current member, who is failing us deeply?"

Rolling my eyes because I work alone.

"No."

Maxton's face distorts in confusion.

"What do you mean, no?"

His nostrils flare. He is easily agitated. Interesting indeed.

"What is your role exactly? A vessel, I heard you say that, but what the fuck does that even mean?"

"Our members confide in me. The Dark One, at the beginning, would give us blackmail to absolve our members' problems. Then as time progressed, as he began to trust us, names started to appear before me. Names of those no longer privileged to live on this earth. I am their Master. They are my people. And together we are The Chapel."

He is charismatic, I see why he is the leader.

"How did you meet my mom?"

His answer will give me everything I need to know.

"Online. I pursued her. She was apprehensive, naturally. But I convinced her the life she was leading wasn't one of happiness and joy. That I could give her everything she needs."

Now, did he learn about me before or after my mom? That remains to be solved.

But for now, I will humor him. Even though I don't believe a fucking word coming from his mouth. Another skill I have is seeing a bullshitter for what they are. And he is that.

"I work alone. I'll give you a list of things I will require. And one of those items on the list will be you staying in your fucking lane. Understood?"

Maxton chuckles, "For a ten-year-old, you sure are ballsy." He thinks I'm amusing. Cute.

"I'm not sure why you're laughing. I am being very fucking serious, Maxton." My tone remains unchanged. He never notices how utterly useless I find him.

"Tonight is the last meeting at the house. Join us. Next time we will be in our new home, the cliffs by the coast."

He turns to leave the closet as I spit back at him, "I'm not wearing those fucking outfits."

Maxton stops in place, not responding. A moment passes as he continues to walk out, leaving me alone again.

I don't trust the fucker. But I will humor him, for now.

FIVE
ELIJAH - AGE TEN

Wearing black jeans with a black hoodie and combat boots, I stand looking out the window facing the backyard. A large fire flickers as maybe twenty followers of The Chapel surround it. They all look like fucking idiots in the black robes and white masks.

Maxton, who is The Master, stands before the flames as they dance. My mom stands behind him as two others stay close.

Who are they?

That will be a task for later this week when I visit his office next time he is out.

"Elijah, my boy, come down here," Maxton shouts.

If he calls me his boy one more time, I will cut his tongue out of his fucking mouth.

I don't move. Openly disobeying him before his

followers, smirking at him instead. My mom is embarrassed, I'm sure, but I don't care.

He continues to look at me for a few moments longer before focusing his attention back on the fire.

That's when I move. On my own, never will I be summoned like that. I do things because I want to, not because I have to. He would be wise to realize this.

Picking up my wooden bat, which is leaning on the wall next to me, I grip it tightly as I begin to walk down the stairs and towards the back door. My bat drags behind me, scratching his precious wood floor. This is how he will learn, do not fucking test me.

Opening the back door, the hinges squeak, catching everyone's attention.

They all look over at me, the cracking of the fire breaks the silence into something somewhat bearable.

"Welcome, Elijah. The Dark One is thrilled that you decided to join us."

SIX

ELIJAH - AGE SIXTEEN

S itting in my black car with black tint, I wait.

My dark hood falls over my face. My teeth play with my lip piercing, which I got a few months ago. I officially got my license last week, but I have been driving alone since I was fourteen. Being associated with the infamous Blackwood cult, The Chapel means people look the other way from me. Except for one. He has been very fucking naughty, and The Dark One conveniently gave his name to Maxton as the next sacrifice at La Notte del Diavolo; Devils Night.

Joe Gregor, he works with the local authorities. He is trying to make a name for himself. He won't be around much longer to do so.

Street lamps line the residential area. Looking down at my watch, it's nearly midnight.

Where is this motherfucker?

Just as I look up, bright headlights reflect in my rearview mirror and turn into his driveway.

Go time.

Getting out of my car, I close the door quietly behind me. Not to raise suspicion, I walk casually towards his home where his car has just now parked. Reaching his driveway before he gets out, I walk up it and lean against his trunk. The door opens quickly. "Hey, who are you?" There is good ol' Joe.

The car moves behind me as he gets out and slams the door. I hear his shoes against the cement as he walks up to me.

Grabbing my shoulder, he pulls me to face him.

Which is the first of many mistakes he makes tonight.

Slowly raising my head, my eyes connect with his. They widen with realization. A sinister smile forms on my face, I fucking love this part.

"Don't move, Joe. If you try to run, I will catch you and make your last moments on this earth un-fucking-bearable. Do you understand?"

The lie flows freely out of my mouth. Either way, I'm going to have fun with him.

His lip trembles as his chest rises with each heavy breath.

Holding my hand out, "Give me your cuffs."

Joe's head shakes like he has a choice.

"Hard or easy? It's up to you how this ends." It's not.

Slowly moving his hand to his holster, I am aware he could grab his gun and shoot me. But I am also very quick. I would turn it around on him before he was able to pull the trigger, resulting in him shooting himself in the head. But it seems like he is being a good little boy for me, he unlatches his cuffs with shaking fingers.

Tired of the waiting, I rip them out of his hand.

"Turn around, place your hands behind your back." Oh, how the tables have turned. He listens, turning slowly on weak knees. The guy is in his mid-thirties and in good shape, with no family. And acting like a complete bitch.

Reaching out, I pull his wrists together and cuff him tightly, not caring if circulation gets cut off and his hands die. I almost prefer it if that did happen, strictly for my own enjoyment.

"The CCTV has been put on a loop. The cameras here and at the other neighbor homes will be rendered useless if your station even bothers to investigate. Which they won't. Because they are far wiser than you, Joe." Taunting him as I push him forward towards my waiting vehicle.

Reaching into my pants pocket, I grip my keys and click the trunk button, it pops open with a dim light shining within it. Lined with clear plastic to not leave stains should this have gone another way.

As we reach it, I push him forward. Losing his balance, he falls face-forward into my trunk. I grab his legs and toss the rest of him in before slamming the trunk closed. Homeboy is in shock. He hasn't screamed once. Perhaps he is saving them all for me later?

Pulling up to The Chapel, I park my car in front of the entrance which is an archway within a giant wall of rock. Just on the other side of this cliff is the ocean. The coast is lined with them, many of which are home to caves and alcoves.

Reaching behind me, I grab my black backpack which carries my supplies needed for this evening, and then my bat which is on my passenger seat. As I get out, I throw the bag over my shoulders and slip the bat through a strap so it hangs off it. Moving to the trunk, I open it. Joe has gotten brave but I expected it, standing back as his feet kick out with a monstrous roar leaving his mouth. Rolling my eyes, I reach forward with my fist tight and punch him on the side of his head, right on the temple. This knocks him out, making him nothing more than dead weight.

Gripping under his armpit, I drag him up and over the lip of the trunk. Dropping him to the dirt ground, I close my trunk before re-gripping him and dragging good ol' Joe into The Chapel.

Torches line the passages, dirt and gravel crunch beneath my boots with each step. There were no other cars here, but I can always count on at least two followers being here watching over the place. Not that they would do anything if anyone did come snooping, but they like to feel tough.

As I turn, Joe's body follows, his heels dragging, leaving a trail behind us. Entering the main space, it's large with unlit white candles surrounding the perimeter, lit torches are on the wall. At the front of the space is a long, dark wood table which is my work-station today. Just behind it is an elevated piece of stone where Maxton rules from and just beside the table is the sacred fire, which they worship.

Throwing Joe on the table, I roll his body so he is on his stomach. Tossing my bag and bat down, I reach for my bolt cutters inside of it and snap the cuffs off.

Dropping my cutter and cuffs to my feet, I roll him back over and begin securing his hands and feet with the leather restraints attached to the table.

As I latch the last one up, excitement begins to lace my veins, this fucker isn't going anywhere.

A tiny voice comes from behind me, "Hi there, Elijah."

Does it look like I am in the mood for small talk?

My tone is uninviting as I shout back, "Fuck off."

I hear footsteps scurry away.

Good.

Walking back to my bag, I look at all my options, *what do I pick first?*

Brushing my fingers over each of my precious tools, I gravitate towards the pliers this time.

Gripping them within my hand, I pull them out, a fucking beautiful piece of steel which is multipurpose. Just how I like it.

Joe is still passed out.

Standing up from my crouched position, I walk over to the long table, which is now Joe's final resting place.

His head is limp, facing me. I grip his jaw and push my thumb and forefinger on either side of his cheek, forcing his mouth open. Shoving the pliers in his mouth, I grip one of his canines with my tool, pulling and wiggling it out of his mouth. The tooth doesn't follow effortlessly, some work is needed as it dislodges from the bone of his jaw and through his pink gums. He immediately starts to bleed as I slide the long root out.

A loud shriek follows.

Excellent, he's awake.

Joe tries to move his head, but I regrip it in my hands, squeezing his jaw, holding him still as I bring his tooth out. Holding it up in front of him, I look down. "Good Morning, Joe. Glad you could join me."

Tears stream down his face. The bitch is already showing how much of a fucking pussy he is.

"Joe, it seems like *"The Dark One"* gave the good leader your name! Which leads us to this moment, right now. Take it in. It will be one of your last moments." An evil chuckle leaves me as I use the term The Dark One loosely.

I fucking love this.

Still holding onto his jaw, blood trickles down his chin onto my hand. It's beautiful, the crimson red against my pale skin ignites a fire within me. My passion is this. I was born to hurt.

Dropping the pliers, the hard steel and his tooth smash on his face, landing directly on his nose. Another painful scream erupts from him, as his nose joins his mouth, bleeding.

Letting go of his chin, I go back to my bag of goodies, this time taking my taser out. Switching it on, I place it against his exposed neck, just above the collar of his uniform shirt and let the sparks fly. Joe's body begins to convulse. The longer I keep it on him, the harder he shakes while his tongue sticks out of his mouth. His teeth bite down on it as his muscles tighten. His body tries to contract now his torso lifts him slightly as he is restrained. Looking down at his body, a wet spot forms by his dick, homeboy has pissed himself.

Looking back up at his face while I keep the device running, his mouth is surrounded by thick blood.

He bit his tongue.

Stopping the electric shock flowing through him, I put the taser down. His body falls limp against the table as I reach up and grip the blood-coated appendage. It is still attached by just a tiny piece of skin and muscle, so I help him by ripping it clean off.

It takes me pushing his forehead backward while

my other hand digs its fingernails into the tongue to grip it, then pulling it with everything I have. Once it's torn clean out of his mouth, more blood follows, gushing down his chin.

Tossing the tongue behind me, I admire my work. And we are only just getting started.

The pig pussy comes in and out of consciousness the entire time I play.

Using scissors, I cut his uniform off him and remove his work belt.

His bare skin is exposed.

With the same scissors, I carve into his stomach, *PIG*.

Then using my hands, I spread the blood coming from the cuts over his chest, like a piece of art, my art. Rubbing it over his erect nipples, into his coarse chest hair, and up his throat.

Joe's eyes lazily open, briefly before closing again.

Rolling my eyes, he's one of the weakest I've had the pleasure of destroying.

I left his boxers on as I have no interest in seeing his small dick or being anywhere around his pissy underpants. His work trousers were bad enough.

The next toy I bring out is a miniature version of a bear trap. I built this myself, as the regular-size one is too big for what I need it for. Pulling it out of my bag, it's in its closed position. Stepping back up to the table where my new pal, Joe lies, I press down on the latch and pry the clamps open. Each side of the clamp is decorated with sharp spikes, so when it closes, it impales whatever it captures.

I think it's time for dear Joe to wake up.

Placing the device over his thigh muscles, I push it down. The pressure of his leg pushing into the flat metal piece in the middle triggers the clamps to close. The spikes penetrate through his skin and muscles, and a loud scream erupts, echoing in the cave.

"Welcome back, Joe!"

Whimpers and mumbles of self-pity exit his mouth. "Why? Why?" Can be faintly made out, thanks to his lack of tongue he can no longer speak properly.

Rolling my eyes, I don't respond.

His leg trembles from the impact. Blood begins to seep out from where the spikes are embedded.

Pride radiates from my chest as I take in the sight before me.

"That's enough, clean this up. Members are starting to arrive." Maxton instructs from behind me.

Before I remove the device, I smile at the idea that enters my head. Reaching down, I grab my bat. Lifting it above my head, I slam it down onto the miniature trap, causing the spikes to move inside his leg and through his muscle. More screams fill the room as I continue to beat down on it.

Before stepping back, I look up at the pathetic sight and slam my bat down against his wrist once, twice, three times. Bones crack as I continue to pound into him, and my vision starts to fade to black. But I stop myself before I can become fully entranced in the moment.

Pulling back, I drop my bat, grab my scissors and pliers, and toss them into my open bag. Next, I unlatched the trap from his leg. As the spikes pull out, more blood erupts from him.

Satisfied, I close it back up and add it back to the bag, doing it up and throwing it over my shoulder. Grabbing my bat next, I turn around and head towards the arched entrance where Maxton still remains.

"Do I need to come back, or will you bleed him out?" I casually ask.

Looking at me, his voice is deep. "No dagger tonight, The Dark One requests he goes slowly. A job well done, Elijah. You can go home."

I don't acknowledge his words, I don't need his praise. I need to kill. I need to torture. It's why I humor this bullshit.

Adrenaline courses through me, I'm not going home.

I'm going to fuck.

SEVEN

ELIJAH - AGE EIGHTEEN

It's no secret in town what I do.

Who I do it for.

And what I am capable of, given the opportunity.

This has automatically made me the center of desperate pussy's attention.

This evening, which has now turned into the early hours of the morning, kept me busy.

Another name, another La Notte del Diavolo.

This one was quick, a follower who turned their back on The Chapel. This one was to send a message to anyone else thinking about it.

Stabbed in the heart.

I left afterward. I don't do clean-up duty after these things. Mind you, I know how, and if I wanted a body to disappear, I could make it happen. But with The Chapel, that's some other bitches job. And typically the bodies go swimming with the sharks.

Adrenaline is high after each kill. My outlet—sex.

Tonight, I have a seemingly desperate brunette riding my cock in the back of my car.

I moved out of Maxton and my mom's place the moment the clock struck midnight on my eighteenth birthday.

The trust fund my dad set up for me kicked in, and I was gone.

I found a place outside of town that's secluded, it's perfect.

I've started working on my in-home version of the shed at my dad's, but it's way fucking better.

I've missed having my place of solitude. I have been stationed in The Chapel for the past eight years with all my gear in my backpack. Now it will have its own home.

That's why I have this chick bouncing on my cock in my car, because I never bring chicks back to my sacred space.

With my black hoodie still on, my jeans are around my knees as the brunette rides my hard cock. Her head is thrown back, her long locks tickle my thighs, and her tits bounce as she rocks on me.

"Fuck, Eli. You feel so good," she whimpers.

"Shut up and milk my cock."

I don't want to hear her or any other desperate slut speak while my cock is in their mouth, pussy, or ass.

She goes from speaking to moaning, which is almost just as bad, but I allow it.

As my climax builds, watching her body move on me, I grip her hips with my hands and take control, pounding into her as hard as I fucking can. The tip of my cock rubs against her cervix with each thrust. Her pussy walls grip around me.

My balls tingle, tightening as my come erupts out of me, filling the condom as I continue to work her, using her for my own release.

Faintly I can still hear her moans, but I am now too absorbed in my own orgasm to hear her. My body tingles, almost like a numb feeling is encompassing me.

Her pussy milks me, as my balls finish emptying.

The feeling comes back into my legs first, the rest of my body follows as my eyes remain hooded.

With a heavy breath, I toss the brunette off me.

"Hey, I wasn't done coming," she complains from the floor of my backseat, her knees lifted to her chest.

"Don't care. I got what I needed. Now get out," I demand as I pull my pants up, keeping the condom on. I don't trust the bitch.

Slipping her tee over her head first, she sits on the edge of the seat, sliding her jean shorts up and over her ass, which I have had a few times now.

She's a decent fuck.

She does the job I need her to do.

Once dressed, she doesn't move. Looking down at her hands, she whispers, "One day, I'm not going to let you do this anymore."

Not bothered, I shrug. "That's fine."

Shaking her head, she looks at me, eyes glaring, "Fuck you, Elijah Sinclair. You are not a good person."

I don't respond, because I already know this.

And I don't fucking care.

She slides her feet into her high-top sneakers and gets out of the car, slamming the door behind her.

Grabbing my phone from my front pocket, I find 'Brunette' in my contacts and delete her from my phone.

Once they start to show signs of attachment, they are done.

No longer in the rotation.

Throwing my phone onto the middle console, I climb through the gap between the seats and get comfortable again in the driver's seat.

Undoing my pants quickly, I pull my cock out and take the soaked condom off. Unrolling my window and tossing it out, letting my come drip out of the rubber onto the ground. Turning my car on, I pull my pants back up and put my car into gear. Slamming down on the gas, my tires spin, squealing as they burn against the cement parking lot. My tail swings before the rest of the car catches up, speeding away into the sunrise.

CHAPTER
EIGHT
ELIJAH - AGE TWENTY

"Son, you know what's coming."

"Yes Dad. Fuck. I've known since I was five."

I respect my dad. We have kept in touch over the ten years that I have been away. But he acts like I don't have a fucking clue what is coming. At any moment, he and the society could call me back, now that I have turned twenty.

I am fucking aware.

His stern voice rumbles through my speaker, "Good. I'll be in touch when it's time."

Then the call disconnects.

I'm sitting in Maxton's home office. I often come in here when he isn't home to see what kind of fun things I can find.

Sometimes it's nothing. Other times, it's different bank statements showing all the money he has conned out of his followers. I don't feel bad. If they are dumb enough to believe him, then let them be dumb enough to fund his lifestyle.

My face is painted in black paint, shaded perfectly like a skull.

This is fucking me.

Take it or leave it. I don't give a flying fuck. Plus, stepdaddy hates it when I do this, which makes me love it more.

My phone vibrates on his desk, speaking of the devil.

I click the green button and put it on speaker, "Yes, Master, how may I be of service?" Sarcasm flows freely from my lips .

"Show some fucking respect. Or have you forgotten who I am?"

Rolling my eyes, he is always this dramatic. "No, I just don't always care."

"Chapel, tonight. And it's not like anything we have had before. Don't be late."

The call ends.

"Why do these fuckers keep hanging up on me?"

Hmm, this is interesting. What does Maxton have up his sleeve for this one?

Walking through the dimly lit hall of The Chapel, torches of fire line either side of me. My bat drags behind, leaving a trail behind me in the gravel as I walk. People will see it and know I'm here, with my preferred weapon of choice.

A few followers in their black robes and white masks rush past me, not wanting to be late.

Kiss asses.

Gravel crunches beneath my boots as I casually walk under the arched entrance to the main room. Crossing my legs, I lean against the cold rock and watch the performance that Maxton is putting on.

The long sleeves of my black zip-up hoodie are pushed up, exposing my tattoo-covered arms. One tattoo is the symbol of The Chapel, the outline of wings. I was graced with the ability to obtain such a tattoo once I turned eighteen. One of the followers inked it on me, as he does for everyone.

I did it to humor Maxton. Again, because I get what I want in return, torture and killing. And he gets what he wants, people he doesn't care for gone.

A win, win some would say.

Taking in the scene before me, it is like any other naming.

The damp cave room is lined with white candles, which are lit, and the room is quiet as Maxton acquires The Chapel's next victim.

All of his followers stand at attention, facing the fire where Maxton stands, looking into it. My mom and his second and third in command stand behind him. They don't go by names, none of them do. They are simply just second and third.

But I know who they are.

Information is power. Observation is key.

The room remains silent for minutes, which feels like hours. I'm not always here for the naming. Sometimes he just calls to let me know who I am getting, which is my preferred method.

He is putting on a show, and it's getting fucking ridiculous.

I am half tempted to use my bat on him and give the people a real show.

Sometimes, I wonder what would happen if I shoved the end of my bat up his ass. Would it splinter inside of him as I slid it out? Causing him to bleed while he screams in agony at the invasion. Would I accidentally go too deep? Compromising his internal organs, perhaps bursting something that is vital? Resulting in internal bleeding and slowly dying without realizing it before it's too late?

So many ideas.

But I would never put my bat anywhere near this fraud's ass.

My bat is worth much more to me than that. But it doesn't stop me from daydreaming about it at every opportunity.

"Ah, Yes. As you wish. We are here to serve you." Maxton's voice invades my happy place as he breaks the silence that was stretched across the space.

My mom's hand reaches up to his shoulder. "Master, tell us, what did The Dark One say?" Her eagerness just proves how weak she is. Always looking to please.

Maxton shrugs her off as he walks toward the elevated rock stage. Standing above and before his followers, he reaches his arms wide while tilting his masked face up toward the jagged rock ceiling.

"The Dark One has given us a gift!" His loud voice echoes, bouncing off the walls. "This coming La Notte del Diavolo, brings us two names. Suzie and Rain Mills."

A loud gasp follows.

Never have I been given two names. Color me suspicious, but I will take it regardless.

Scrunching my brows and tilting my head. Come to think of it, I have never heard of these two before. What's his motive here?

"Elijah has the names. He will bring them to us for our next La Notte del Diavolo!"

Loud cheers and clapping erupt as excitement fills the space.

As I stand to leave, his powerful voice stops me. "Elijah, please stay behind. We have many things to discuss. The rest of you, be free."

I salute him and step further inside, leaning against the rock wall, so the excited cult members can exit the area.

They file out in an orderly fashion, a sea of black robes moves past me. Some whisper, wondering what is coming next, and what does all this mean?

As the last one leaves, I don't move.

If he wants to talk, he can come to me.

Maxton turns to face his inner circle, "Two, Three, Wife, you are also dismissed." The three of them scurry away, also exiting through the same archway.

He shakes his head as he notices that I don't move.

Which also shouldn't shock him.

He steps down onto the ground and makes his way over to me.

"This task is very important. The next La Notte del Diavolo, isn't for a month. There is ground work that needs to be done before you take these two and bring them to us."

Nodding, I say, "Go on."

"I have an address, they are a couple of towns over. First, you need to get to Rain. We need a sample of her hair or anything that could give us her DNA to be tested."

The fuck is this?

"Over twenty-one years ago, I had relations with Suzie. Rain is most likely mine, and I have been watching from a distance. Her birthday is a month away, it's time she comes home to me, to us, The Chapel, if she is in fact, mine."

"And Suzie?" I question, what is his end game here?

"If Rain is mine and I was robbed of being her father, Suzie will be sacrificed to The Dark One. Do you understand?"

Nodding my head, I absorb everything he is telling me.

"You have two weeks to confirm she is mine. If she is, we take them both on Rain's twenty-first birthday and as a reward for all your hard work, Rain will be yours."

Mine?

I've never been given anyone as a gift before.

Well, not in this capacity. To have such a responsibility.

"Send me the details. I will get started tomorrow." I remain neutral in my response, not wanting to show my excitement.

He pats my shoulder. "Of course." Then walks away, ending the conversation.

I am left in the room alone.

Looking into the fire, the yellows, reds, and oranges hypnotize me as they dance before me.

Rain Mills.

My new obsession.

Her room smells of the fresh flowers on her dresser, which appear to have been picked from her front garden.

After taking what I need for the DNA test, I snoop around her room, of course.

A few pictures of her and her mom decorate the space.

She is fucking gorgeous. The obsession became more real as I took her in.

The feeling of her presence in that room was strong. Standing over her bed, it felt like she was almost there with me, as if I were looking down at her sleeping.

I can feel it.

Her energy matches mine, but it has never been given the opportunity like mine to come out and shine.

The need to protect is new to me. But for her, I will do it.

She is still too innocent for this world, but I plan to change that.

Stepping back, a picture of her on her nightstand catches my eye, dark black hair, hazel eyes, and a bright smile stares back at me. Delicate pale skin and her cute nose.

Picking up the cheap plastic white frame, my finger traces along her face.

Captivated.

She is mine.

I just got back into town.

Impulse took over, and now I am here at the tattoo shop, which also does my piercings.

I'm giving her something no one else has had. Something that is truly and only hers.

Rain possesses me.

I am all fucking hers.

Shane's annoying voice interrupts my thoughts, "You can't fuck for a few weeks after you do this."

Laying on the piercing table, my soft cock hangs out of my pants. "I don't care, just do it."

My tone is short and impatient.

I won't be fucking anyone else ever again.

She won't be mine for a couple more weeks. It's plenty of time for it to heal.

His gloved hands grip me. He was going to use a clamp, but I told him to man up, it's just a dick.

My eyes focus on his movements as the thick, large needle pierces through my sensitive head.

I know my pupils are dilated. It happens when I play with my human toys, and I am experiencing the same feeling with this.

Excitement, the thrill, it's fucking beautiful.

He reaches for the barbell jewelry and pushes it behind the needle, following it through my cock.

The needle finishes threading through my flesh, and the end of the barbell joins as he twists the ball on tightly.

As he finishes cleaning off the area, which barely even bled, I think about how my entire life was leading up to this moment.

My mind and body have never reacted this way to

another human, these feelings are unfamiliar and uncomfortable. Her name has ignited something inside of me. Woken a beast I didn't know was there. This beast isn't like my others. It causes warmth in my chest just by thinking of her.

Then the need to see her and be near her takes over.

Sitting up, I grip the waist of my jeans and quickly slide them up my legs, and I hop down off the table.

"Dude, chill. Be gentle. You don't want that shit getting caught on anything. It will fucking hurt like nothing you have felt before," my piercer warns.

Ignoring him, I finish doing up my jeans and reach into my pants pocket for my cash. I toss a couple hundred dollar bills on the bed behind me and leave.

He's used to me.

But this is not something that I am used to.

The overwhelming urgency.

And it all stems from a name.

Rain Mills.

You are coming home.

You. Are. Mine.

The End.

Acknowledgments

As promised the year of Elijah Sinclair continues!

Thank you to my incredible team and readers. I fucking adore you.

My Alpha and Betas - Twisted Kait, Ariana, Ashley, T (Tiesha), Boss (Jay Depraved), Hayley and Ms. Martha Moo Moo (Amy)

To the year of Elijah, cheers little bats!

xx
kins

About the Author

Kinsley is a Canadian, Dark Romance Author who dabbles in Taboo, Forbidden, and is currently in her Horror Era. When she isn't plotting her next twisted book or watching true crime docs with her cats, you can find her working for the man. Reading. Or drinking wine while causing chaos with friends, let's not limit ourselves now. Make sure you follow Kins on her socials and sign up for her newsletter to see what is coming next!

authorkinsleykincaid.com

More from the Author

FORBIDDEN
Let's Play
Within the Shadows
Lessons from the Depraved
Haunted by the Devil; The Devil's Society
Sinner; The Devil's Society
Homecoming; The Devil's Society
Unholy; The Devil's Society - 2025

TABOO
Wrecked
Sutton Asylum
Dark Temptation: Part One
Ghost Dick; A Port Canyon Chronicle
Dark Temptation: Part Two
Lessons; An Extremely Fucking Taboo Extended
Epilogue

Sick Obsession - Coming 2024
Dark Temptation: Part Three 2025
Fuck Me, Daddy; A Port Canyon Chronicle - TBD
Taboo ebooks, audio & paperbacks can be ordered directly via the authors' website. Paperbacks ship direct from printer